For Tom

Published by Dial Books for Young Readers
A division of Penguin Young Readers Group
345 Hudson Street
New York, New York 10014

Designed by Nancy R. Leo-Kelly
Text set in Perpetua
Manufactured in China on acid-free paper
1 3 5 7 9 10 8 6 4 2

Library of Congress Cataloging-in-Publication Data
Sneed, Brad.
Thumbelina / story by Hans Christian Andersen ;
adapted and illustrated by Brad Sneed.
p. cm.
Summary: After being kidnapped by a toad, a beautiful girl no bigger than
a thumb has many adventures and makes many animal friends
before meeting the perfect mate just her size.
ISBN 0-8037-2812-3
[1. Fairy tales.] I. Andersen, H. C. (Hans Christian), 1805–1875.
Tommelise. English. II. Title.
PZ8.S4145Th 2004   [E]—dc22   2003013164

The artwork for this book was created with watercolors on watercolor paper.

Thumbelina

story by HANS CHRISTIAN ANDERSEN

adapted and illustrated by Brad Sneed

Dial Books for Young Readers New York

Once there was a woman who wanted very much to have a child, but as the years passed, her wish was never granted. At last she went to visit an old witch to ask for her help. Patiently the witch listened and then replied, "Take this seed and plant it in a flowerpot. But beware, for strong magic will never do exactly as you desire."

The woman thanked the witch and hurried home. She planted the seed and watered it carefully. Immediately a lovely flower sprang up, though its petals stayed tightly closed.

The woman was terribly disappointed, but said, "It *is* a beautiful flower," and she kissed the petals. As soon as she did, the flower opened to reveal a very tiny girl sitting inside. In fact, the child was scarcely as tall as the woman's thumb, and so she named her "Thumbelina."

Thumbelina was so little, she was able to use a walnut shell for a bed and flower petals for a mattress. During the day she played on a table, where the woman placed a dish full of water. A large tulip petal became her boat and the tiny girl rowed from side to side, with two oars made of horsehair. While she rowed, Thumbelina sang more sweetly than anything that had ever before been heard.

One night, a big toad crept through an open window and leaped onto the table where Thumbelina was sleeping. "What a pretty wife she would make for my son!" said the toad, and she took up the walnut shell and jumped through the window into the garden.

The toad lived with her son on the muddy bank of a nearby stream. When he saw Thumbelina, the son began to croak excitedly.

"Hush, or you'll wake her," said the mother toad. "Then she might run away! Now, help me put her on one of the lily pads. She's so very small, it will seem like an island to her and she'll never be able to escape. Quickly, and then we must prepare your new home under the marsh."

Early the next morning Thumbelina woke, and was startled to find herself on a lily pad in the middle of a stream. She could see nothing but water on every side of the large green leaf and no way of reaching land. She began to cry for help, until at last the mother toad swam out to the lily pad with her son.

The old toad said, "Hush, child. I want you to meet my son. He is to be your husband and you will live happily together under the marsh."

"Croak, croak, croak," was all her son could say for himself. Then the toads stole Thumbelina's walnut shell bed and swam away, for they were still not finished with their preparations.

As soon as they were out of sight, Thumbelina began to cry louder for help. Fortunately the fish who swam in the water had heard everything. It made them sorry to think that the poor girl must go and live with the horrible toads. They nibbled away at the lily stalk until Thumbelina's leaf was set free and started to drift downstream.

Thumbelina sailed past many towns, and was happy, for now the toads could not possibly catch her, and she enjoyed feeling the warm sunshine on her face. A butterfly fluttered around her, and at last lighted on her lily pad. Thumbelina gave one end of her sash to the butterfly and fastened the other end to the lily pad, which now glided faster than ever.

As they neared a bend in the stream, suddenly a large beetle flew by. *Whoosh!* The moment he caught sight of Thumbelina, he grabbed her and flew to a tree.

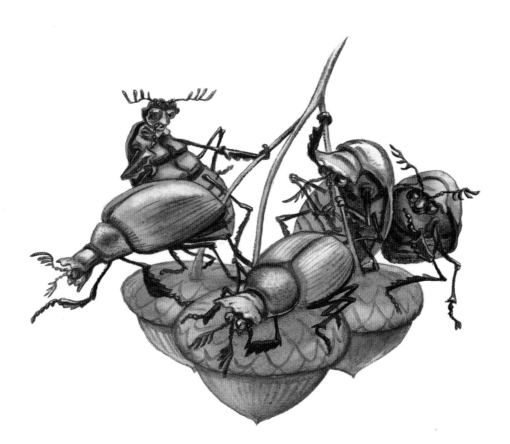

Thumbelina cried out, and begged him to let her go. But the beetle seated himself by her side, gave her some honey to eat, and told her she was very pretty, though not in the least like an insect. Meanwhile all the beetles who lived in the tree stared curiously at Thumbelina, and turned up their feelers at her.

One said, "She has only two legs. How ugly that looks!"

"She has no feelers," said another.

"She looks just like a human being. Oh, she is ugly!" they all exclaimed.

The beetle who had captured Thumbelina listened to the others, growing more dejected with each insult. Finally he decided he would have no more to do with her. He flew Thumbelina down from the tree and dropped her on a daisy. Surprised but unharmed, Thumbelina began to laugh, happy to be free again.

That summer Thumbelina lived all alone in the forest. She wove herself a bed of grass, and hung it under a wide leaf to protect herself from the rain. She ate honey from the flowers, and drank the dew from their leaves every morning.

But as autumn days turned to winter, all the birds who had sung to her flew away. The leaves on the trees turned brown. Soon it began to snow, and the snowflakes, as they fell upon her, were like a whole shovelful falling upon one of us, for we are tall while she was only two inches high.

Near the woods lay a large cornfield, but only the dry stubble remained. Still, for Thumbelina it was like struggling through a large wood. Oh, how she shivered with the cold! She came at last to the door of a field mouse, who lived in a snug underground den. Thumbelina knocked timidly to beg for a morsel of food.

"You poor little creature," said the field mouse. "Come into my warm den and have something to eat." The mouse was so pleased to have company that she said, "You're welcome to stay with me all winter, if you like. But you must keep my rooms clean and neat, and sing songs for me, for I love to hear music." Thumbelina did everything the field mouse asked, and began to feel very comfortable in her new home.

"We'll have a visitor soon," said the field mouse one day. "My neighbor the mole is stopping by. He is even better off than I am. If you could only have him for a husband, you would be well provided for indeed."

But when the mole came to visit, Thumbelina discovered that she did not care for him at all. He preferred being underground, did not like the sun, or the blue sky, or even the flowers, and seemed very grumpy.

After supper the mole invited Thumbelina and the field mouse to take an evening stroll, using the long passage he had dug to his own dwelling. Halfway along they came across a dead swallow. The mole pushed it aside and said, "How dreadful to be a bird. It can't even survive the winter." The field mouse loudly agreed, but Thumbelina kept silent. When the two others had turned their backs, she gently stroked the bird's feathers. "Little swallow, is it you who sang to me this summer?" she whispered. But then the field mouse said they must be getting home, as it was growing late.

During the night Thumbelina could not stop thinking of the swallow. She crept out of bed, and wove a large blanket out of hay. Then she carried it to the dead bird and spread it over him.

"Poor thing," she said, and rested her head on the bird's breast, only to hear something inside the bird go *thump, thump*. It was the bird's heart! He was not really dead—only frozen with cold.

"Thank you, dear girl," said the weak swallow. "I feel so warm that I think I will soon be able to fly."

"Oh, no," said she. "It's snowing outside now. Rest and I will take care of you until you are well again."

That whole winter the swallow remained underground while Thumbelina nursed him, though she never dared tell the mole or the field mouse, for they did not like swallows or any other kind of bird.

At last it was spring and the swallow felt well
enough to fly. Thumbelina opened a hole in the
roof of the tunnel, and the sun shone in. As he
prepared for his journey, the swallow invited her
to go with him. But Thumbelina knew it would
make the field mouse very sad if she left, and so
she said no.

"I will miss you," said the swallow,
and away he flew. Thumbelina felt tears
spring to her eyes, but dutifully she
returned to her chores.

Late that summer the field mouse announced, "I have wonderful news, Thumbelina. The mole has asked to marry you. What a lucky day for a humble child like you! I have already hired four spiders to weave the lace for your wedding gown."

"I cannot marry the mole," said Thumbelina. "I do not love him."

"Nonsense," replied the field mouse. "Don't be pig-headed. He is a very handsome mole. The queen herself does not wear more beautiful velvets and furs. You ought to be thankful for such good fortune." And though Thumbelina protested, the mouse would hear no more complaints.

The poor girl was very unhappy and wanted to run away. But she knew winter was coming and she might freeze in the forest. And so she stood at the door for her last glimpse of the summer flowers.

Suddenly she heard her old friend the swallow calling to her from the sky. He landed at her doorstep, and Thumbelina poured out her troubles to him.

"I am about to make my winter journey to warmer lands," said the swallow. "Will you join me this time?"

"Yes, I will!" said Thumbelina. And she climbed up onto the bird's back.

The swallow rose in the air and flew over the forest and the mountains, then high above the sea, until they reached the warm countries, where trees were heavy with fruit, and the air fragrant with flower blossoms.

Finally they came to a lake, where there stood the ruins of an old palace. Vines clustered around its pillars, and at the top were many swallows' nests.

"Here is my home," said the swallow. "But for you, there are the flowers below. Would you like to choose one as your new home?" The swallow flew down and Thumbelina slid from his back onto a large flower. How surprised she was to see, in the middle of that very flower, a tiny little man! He had a crown on his head, and delicate wings at his shoulders, and was not much larger than Thumbelina herself.

"Oh, how wonderful he is!" whispered Thumbelina to the swallow.

At first the little king was frightened by the bird, who appeared like a giant to him. But when he saw Thumbelina, he was enchanted. He asked her name, and if she would stay and perhaps one day be his wife, the queen of all the flowers.

This certainly was a very different sort of husband from the son of the toad, or the disagreeable mole. So Thumbelina said yes to the handsome king with the kind face, and she took his hand. Then all the flowers opened and out of every one came more tiny people. Each of them brought Thumbelina a gift, but the best was a pair of wings so that she too could fly from flower to flower. Then there was much rejoicing, and the swallow sang to them about Thumbelina and her adventures.

When winter came to an end, it was time for the swallow to say farewell and make his yearly journey back to Denmark. There he had a nest over the window of a house in which lived a writer of fairy tales. And every evening, as the sun would set, the swallow sang, "Tweet, tweet," and from his song came this very story.

The End